W9-BCI-953

A Grandma Like Yours

by Andria Warmflash Rosenbaum
illustrated by Barb Björnson

For Savta and Saba Warmflash
and
Bubbe and Zayde Rosenbaum,
each a grandchild's wish!
— A.W.R

To Matta, a very loving Amma and dear friend,
and
Mabel who has love in her heart for all of us.
— B.K.B.

A ***bubbe***, a **savta**
No two are the same
Each **GRANDMA** is special
Whatever her name.

Do **elephant grannies** remember by heart

Each grandchild's name without keeping a chart?

Do **chimpanzee nanas** bake challah from scratch

Then lace up their
sneakers to have
a quick catch?

Does a **kangaroo savta** like dancing the horah

Preparing to light her silver menorah?

Can **bow~wowing bubbes** wear Purim disguises

Delivering baskets of
yummy surprises?

Does a **grandma giraffe** do a mitzvah a day

Bringing soup to the sick
with a rose on the tray?

Do **grandmother bunnies** make seders each year

For 23 cousins all equally dear?

You may call her bubbe or
savta or nanny
Whatever you call her,
she's your favorite granny.

A grandpa, a zayde, a saba, a pop
Your grandpa is certain
to come out on top.

Outside in the
sun in dirt up
to their knees?

Do **grandpas of groundhogs** plant Tu B'Shevat trees

When grandlambs' teeth chatter
because it's too cool?

Do **zaydes of sheep** share their tallit in shul

By counting the minutes
that it has been baking?

Do **porcupine papas** help with matzah-making

In Israel's honor with banners they made?

Do zebras have **zaydes** who love to parade

. . . **snail sabas,** too?

Can they mix up a kugel
that's tasty to chew?

But what about **quail sabas . . .**

So ears young and
old hear the call
loud and clear?

Do **sabas of llamas** blow shofar each year

A ***zayde***, a **saba**
No two are the same
Each **GRANDPA** is special
Whatever his name.

GLOSSARY

Bubbe – grandma (Yiddish)

Challah – Sabbath bread

Horah – Israeli folkdance

Kugel – pudding

Menorah – candelabra used on Hanukkah

Matzah – unleavened bread eaten on Passover

Mitzvah – good deed

Purim – holiday commemorating Queen Esther's rescue of the Jews

Saba – grandpa (Hebrew)

Savta – grandma (Hebrew)

Seder – ritual meal at Passover

Shofar – ram's horn blown on High Holidays

Shul – synagogue

Tallit – prayer shawl

Tu B'Shevat – birthday of the trees

Zayde – grandpa (Yiddish)

Text copyright © 2006 by Andrea Warmflash Rosenbaum
Illustrations copyright © 2006 by Barb Björnson

All rights reserved. International copyright secured. No part of this book may be reproduced, stored in a retrieval system, or transmitted in any form or by any means—electronic, mechanical, photocopying, recording, or otherwise—without the prior written permission of Lerner Publishing Group, Inc., except for the inclusion of brief quotations in an acknowledged review.

Kar-Ben Publishing
A division of Lerner Publishing Group, Inc.
241 First Avenue North
Minneapolis, MN 55401 U.S.A.
1-800-4-KARBEN

Website address: www.karben.com

Library of Congress Cataloging-in-Publication Data

Rosenbaum, Andria Warmflash, 1958–
A grandma like yours ; A grandpa like yours / by Andria Warmflash Rosenbaum : illustrations by Barb Björnson.
p. cm.
Titles from separate title pages; works issued back-to-back and inverted.
Summary: Two rhyming stories of wonderful Jewish grandmothers and grandfathers.
ISBN-13: 978–1–58013–167–4 (lib. bdg. : alk. paper)
ISBN-10: 1–58013–167–0 (lib. bdg. : alk. paper)
1. Upside-down books—Specimens. [1. Grandmothers—Fiction. 2. Grandfathers—Fiction. 3. Jews—Fiction. 4. Stories in rhyme. 5. Upside-down books. 6. Toy and movable books.] I. Björnson, Barbara, 1952– ill. II. Rosenbaum, Andria Warmflash, 1958– Grandpa like yours. III. Title. IV. Title : Grandpa like yours.
PZ8.3.R72245Gra 2006
[E]—dc22 2005004480

Manufactured in the United States of America
4 5 6 7 8 9 – DP – 13 12 11 10 09 08

A Grandpa Like Yours

by Andria Warmflash Rosenbaum
illustrated by Barb Björnson